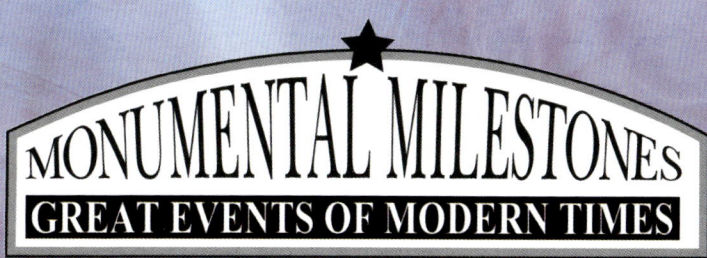

The Dawn of Aviation
The Story of the Wright Brothers

Soaring over the ground at Kitty Hawk, *The Flyer* had a wingspan of just over 40 feet.

Mitchell Lane
PUBLISHERS

P.O. Box 196
Hockessin, Delaware 19707

Titles in the Series

**The Dawn of Aviation:
The Story of the Wright Brothers**

Pearl Harbor and the War with Japan

**Breaking the Sound Barrier:
The Story of Chuck Yeager**

**Top Secret: The Story of the
Manhattan Project**

The Story of the Holocaust

The Civil Rights Movement

**Exploring the North Pole:
The Story of Robert Edwin
Peary and Matthew Henson**

The Story of the Great Depression

**The Cuban Missile Crisis:
The Cold War Goes Hot**

The Fall of the Berlin Wall

**Disaster in the Indian Ocean,
Tsunami, 2004**

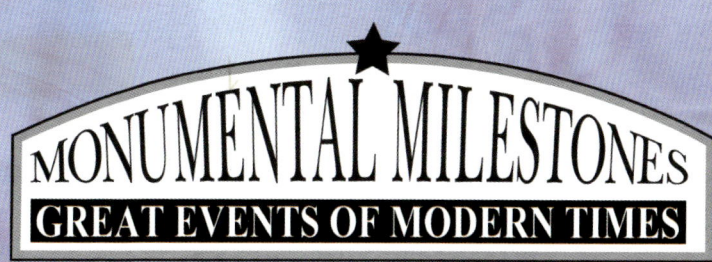

The Dawn of Aviation
The Story of the Wright Brothers

Soaring over the ground at Kitty Hawk, *The Flyer* had a wingspan of just over 40 feet.

Tamra Orr

Copyright © 2005 by Mitchell Lane Publishers, Inc. All rights reserved. No part of this book may be reproduced without written permission from the publisher. Printed and bound in the United States of America.

Printing   1   2   3   4   5   6   7   8

Library of Congress Cataloging-in-Publication Data
Orr, Tamra.
  The dawn of aviation: the story of the Wright brothers / by Tamra Orr.
     p. cm. — (Monumental milestones : great events of modern times)
  Includes bibliographical references and index.
  ISBN 1-58415-396-2 (library bound)
1. Wright, Orville, 1871-1948—Juvenile literature. 2. Wright, Wilbur, 1867-1912—Juvenile literature. 3. Aeronautics—United States—Biography—Juvenile literature. 4. Inventors—United States—Biography—Juvenile literature. I. Title II. Monumental milestones.
TL540.W70775 2005
629.13'0092'273—dc22
                                                                                    2004030308

ABOUT THE AUTHOR: Tamra Orr is a full time writer and author living in the Pacific Northwest. She has written more than 50 educational books for children and families, including *The Biography of Notable Hispanic-Americans*, *School Violence: Halls of Hope Halls of Fear*, and *The Journey of Lewis and Clark*. She is a regular writer for more than 50 national magazines and a dozen standardized testing companies. Orr is mother to four, ages 9 to 21 and life partner to Joseph.

PHOTO CREDITS: Cover, pp. 1, 3, 6 Library of Congress; p. 10 Corbis; pp. 12, 15 Library of Congress; p. 18 Corbis; pp. 26, 34 Library of Congress; p. 37 Jamie Kondrchek; p. 39 Library of Congress; p. 41 Corbis

PUBLISHER'S NOTE: This story is based on the author's extensive research, which she believes to be accurate. Documentation of such research is contained on page 46.

The internet sites referenced herein were active as of the publication date. Due to the fleeting nature of some web sites, we cannot guarantee they will all be active when you are reading this book.

Contents

The Dawn of Aviation
The Story of the Wright Brothers

Tamra Orr

Chapter 1	A Simple Gift, A Grand Notion	7
	FYInfo*: The Father of Flying Models	9
Chapter 2	An Encouraging Environment	11
	FYInfo: Their Little Sister	17
Chapter 3	To Reach the Sky	19
	FYInfo: A Look at the Competition	25
Chapter 4	Success and Beyond	27
	FYInfo: Women in the Air	33
Chapter 5	Protecting Patents and Winning Arguments	35
	FYInfo: The Aerial Experiment Association	42
Chronology		43
Timeline in History		44
Chapter Notes		45
For Further Reading		46
	For Young Adults	46
	Works Consulted	46
	On the Internet	46
Glossary		47
Index		48

*For Your Information

The Wright brothers were inseparable for almost their entire lives.

Taken around 1909, this photograph shows Orville (right) and Wilbur (left) months after Orville had been injured in a crash. He was finally healed enough to return to traveling with his brother, who was his best friend.

A Simple Gift, A Grand Notion

Wilbur and Orville looked out the window again. There was still no sign of their father. Would he ever get here?

The brothers, along with their three siblings Katherine, Lorin, and Reuchlin, were used to their father being gone. As the minister for the Church of the United Brethren in Christ, Milton Wright traveled often. He would journey all the way to the west coast to visit other congregations, and although his children missed him, he frequently brought home a toy or other gifts for them. The anticipation of that toy was what kept Wilbur, eleven, and Orville, seven, running to look out the front window.

Suddenly, there was a sound on the front porch steps. Yes! Father was home. Although he was a stern man, Milton loved his children deeply. Seeing Orville and Wilbur's eager eyes, he pulled out the toy he had hidden behind his back. With a quick flip of the wrist, he sent it flying across the room. The boys were astonished. What had their father given them?

"Late in the autumn of 1878," Wilbur recalled in his diaries, "our father came into the house one evening with some object concealed in his hands, and before we could see what it was, he tossed it into the air. Instead of falling to the floor, as we expected, it flew across the room till it struck the ceiling, where it fluttered awhile and finally sank

CHAPTER 1   A Simple Gift, A Grand Notion

to the floor . . . A toy so delicate lasted only a short time in the hands of small boys, but its memory was abiding."[1]

A quick inspection showed that it was a flying toy called *The Bat*, made out of thin cork, bamboo, paper, and rubber bands. The boys had heard of this unusual toy. It was an invention of a young Frenchman named Alphonse Penaud. In 1878, everyone was talking about them. The boys immediately began twisting the rubber band and letting the toy fly. Each time, it flew almost fifty feet.

The rest of the evening, as well as the rest of the week and beyond, Orville and Wilbur played with their new flying machine. As toys will do—especially those with paper wings—it broke now and then and each time, the boys repaired it. Using it as a model, they also began building bigger forms. To their disappointment, the bigger ones looked great but would not fly.

"We built a number of copies of this toy," recalled Orville in his diaries, "which flew successfully. But when we undertook to fly the toy on a much larger scale, it failed to work so well. The reason for this was not understood by us at the time, so we finally abandoned the experiment."[2]

No one realized, least of all Orville and Wilbur, that their inability to make the larger toy fly and the mystery behind it would turn into their lives' work and inspiration. From a very simple toy would soon come a truly grand notion.

FYInfo
For Your Information

THE FATHER OF FLYING MODELS

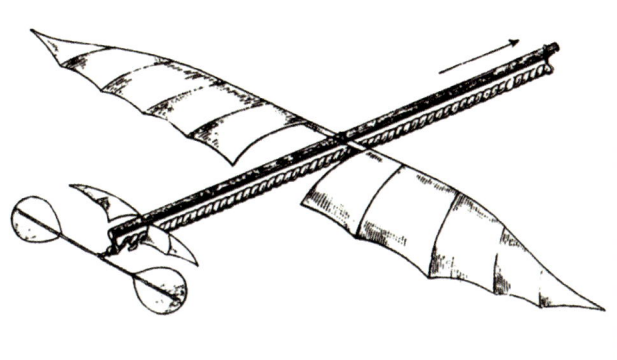

A Drawing of a Planophore

Alphonse Penaud's (1850-1880) plans were in ashes. After years of looking forward to joining the Navy as a marine engineer, a severe illness had made his dream impossible. Not sure what to do with his life now, he decided to pursue the possibility of flight. He thought perhaps he could be the first man to invent a truly working flying machine.

After years of studying, thinking, experimenting, and learning, Penaud did indeed create the world's first heavier-than-air flying machine. His, however, was made out of rubber bands and paper. It had a wing, tail, and propeller in the rear. He called it the "Planophore" and at age 21, he flew it in front of a large crowd at the Tuileries Gardens in Paris, France. They were amazed. His simple toy flew an incredible 181 feet in just eleven seconds. Three years later, Penaud invented a rubber-band-powered helicopter. It had rotating propellers on the top and bottom. It was not long before the young man was being called "The Father of Flying Models."

In 1875, the French Academy of Sciences gave him a prize for his inventions, but Penaud was not satisfied. He wanted to move beyond toys and create an actual flying machine capable of holding a human pilot. Partnering with a mechanic named Paul Gauchot, the two of them filed for a patent to build a full-scale airplane. For four years, Gauchot and Penaud searched for the money to start building their vision. Unfortunately, this was yet another dream that did not come true. Penaud committed suicide before his plans were anything more than drawings on a page.

The Wright's younger sister Katherine was a huge part of their lives.

Katherine gave them encouragement, advice, and support whenever they needed it. The three of them often traveled together and here are on the deck of a ship sailing to France.

An Encouraging Environment

Looking back at all the Wright Brothers accomplished, it is hard to believe they did not have college degrees or any special training in mechanics. They never even graduated from high school. Most likely their ability to understand, adapt, and repair anything mechanical came from their mother, Susan Catherine Koerner.

As a child, Susan had spent a great deal of time in her father's workshop. He was a farmer and a carriage maker and he took the time to teach her how to use the different tools and do simple repairs. This was a talent that Susan needed because Milton could not drive a nail straight into a piece of wood.

The Wright children always knew they could count on their mother to mend whatever was broken or to create a new toy if they needed one. Once she made a sled for her children that was used for years, and now and then, she even made her own appliances for the kitchen. A quiet person, she respected her children's creativity enormously, always carefully picking up any little invention they had left out and putting it in a safe place. Although Milton did not share this inventing ability, he also appreciated it. Orville once wrote, "We were lucky enough to grow up in a home environment where there was always much encouragement to children to pursue intellectual interests, to investigate whatever aroused curiosity. In a different kind of

CHAPTER 2 — An Encouraging Environment

Orville and Wilbur's childhood home was located at 7 Hawthorn Street in Dayton, Ohio.

They had moved there from a small farm near the city of Millville, Indiana. Orville and Katherine were born in this home.

environment," he added, "our curiosity might have been nipped long before it could have borne fruit."[1]

The Wright family was a large one. Susan had seven children; five lived. Reuchlin (pronounced ROOSH-lin) was born in 1861. His brother Lorin followed in 1862 and Wilbur was born in 1867. Twins Otis and Ida were born in 1870 but died shortly after. Orville arrived in 1871 and daughter Katherine in 1874.

The Wright family moved quite often while the children were young, but it was their house at 7 Hawthorn Street in Dayton, Ohio that most of them considered home. Wilbur and Orville were often thought of as twins, as they did everything together. They actually looked nothing

The Dawn of Aviation

alike and their personalities were quite different. Wilbur was quiet, intense, and energetic. He was an excellent student. Orville, on the other hand, was a talker. He was outgoing and friendly, always looking on the bright side of things and the first to tell a joke. While Wilbur was often an oily, dirty mess from whatever invention they were tinkering with at the time, Orville was always quiet, neat, and clean.

Despite their differences, the two brothers could not have been closer. That bond would continue throughout the rest of their lives. When they worked on a project together, they would often begin whistling and humming the exact same song, at the exact same time. Wilbur once wrote, "My brother Orville and myself lived together, played together, worked together, and in fact, thought together. We usually owned all of our toys in common," he added, "talked over our thoughts and aspirations so that nearly everything that was done in our lives has been the result of conversations, suggestions, and discussions between us."[2]

Wilbur, looking for a way to make some money, decided to make and sell kites to his friends. For some reason, his kites seemed to fly higher and faster than any others. What was his secret? Since he did not have a lot of cash for supplies, he cut the wooden ribs for the kites very, very thin in order to make his wood last longer. Those extra thin ribs bent in the wind, allowing the kite to curve and fly higher and faster.

The next project for the brothers was designing and running their own printing press. Amazingly, they constructed one out of a tombstone for the press bed, wheels and cogs from a local junkyard, and the folding top of an old baby buggy they found in the barn. A local printer came to see their press and friend Ed Sines remembered how the man was puzzled by it. "He went into the press room, stood by the machine, looked at it, then sat down beside it and finally crawled underneath it.

CHAPTER 2   An Encouraging Environment

After he had been under the machine some little time," continued Sine, "he got up and said, 'Well, it works, but I certainly don't see how.' "[3]

Despite its primitive construction, the Wright Brothers' press worked, printing up to one thousand pages an hour. They began printing newsletters for their father's church, as well as business cards, advertisements, and brochures for local stores. The business grew enough that Wilbur dropped out of high school in his senior year to run it full time. He had briefly considered going to Yale University to be a minister like his father but it was not meant to be. One day, while playing "shinney," the street version of hockey, he was struck in the face by a teammate. His front teeth were knocked out and he had to have surgery to repair the damage to his face. Although he recovered, he had lost the self-confidence he needed to take off for college and instead returned to the printing business.

In 1889, Orville joined him in the print shop. The two found they worked together wonderfully, even though part of the time was frequently spent arguing loudly. Wilbur once said, "I love to scrap with Orv; he's such a good scrapper."[4] They had a natural way of bouncing ideas off of each other and together, their two minds attacked one problem and solved it. Neither of the boys ever graduated from high school. For a year, they published a four-page community newspaper called *The West Side News*. They tried to turn it into a daily newspaper, but could not compete against the larger publishers and gave up.

While Orville and Wilbur were learning how to run the printing business, their mother's health was failing. For the last two years of her life, she was bedridden and in 1889, she died of a disease called tuberculosis. Katherine was put in charge of the entire household at the age of fourteen and the family struggled to find a way to manage without Susan's presence in the house.

The Dawn of Aviation

In this drawing a woman is shown on a three-wheeler, while the gentlemen follow on high-wheelers. The Wright brothers loved riding bikes and it was not long before they were selling, renting, and repairing them in their own shop.

Bicycles were all the fashion in the late 1890s and early 1900s.

It was not long before the two brothers were caught up in a new fad that was sweeping the nation. While they continued to work on their printing press, they also went out and purchased the latest thing in transportation: the bicycle. While Wilbur preferred to take his bike on long, quiet rides in the country, Orville liked to race his. Between the two of them, they learned a great deal about how bicycles worked, and how to repair them when something went wrong. When other people began to ask them to fix their bikes, once again the Wright Brothers were in business.

Orville and Wilbur's printing business was moved to the top floor of the building they owned and the Wright Cycle Company moved in on

CHAPTER 2   An Encouraging Environment

the main floor. At first, the brothers only sold, repaired, and rented out bicycles. Intrigued by how they worked, however, it was not long before they also began building them. It was not unusual for one of them to sit down, design, and produce a special part if it was needed. Business boomed and they opened several more stores. The printing business was abandoned as the Wright Brothers discovered their fascination for learning about how things moved and how to make them do it faster and better. At the same time, they built their own darkroom for developing the growing number of photographs they were taking.

Everyone in the community knew that the Wright Brothers were good at problem solving. It would not be long before they saw them tackle another new idea. This time it would be one that had captivated the minds and imaginations of the entire world—the possibility of flight.

FYInfo

FOR YOUR INFORMATION

THEIR LITTLE SISTER

Katherine Wright

Even though she was the youngest in the family, Katherine Wright carried a great deal of responsibility on her shoulders from the time she was a teenager. Along with keeping the house running after her mother's death, she helped take care of her father and brothers. Katherine, Orville, and Wilbur were exceptionally close from an early age and the boys often called her *swesterchen* or "little sister" in German.

Most of Katherine's entire life was dedicated to helping her brothers succeed. She helped in their print shop, bicycle store, and with their flying machines. Although she did go to college and hold a job as a teacher, she quit in order to help her family. She did not marry until she was 52 years old, knowing that it would upset her family. She was right. When she finally did marry, Wilbur refused to attend her wedding and did not speak to Katherine again until she was dying two years later.

Orville once wrote of his sister, "When the world speaks of the Wrights, it must include our sister. Much of our effort has been inspired by her."[5]

In 1981, the Gates Learjet Corporation established the Katherine Wright Memorial Award to be given out once a year to the woman who either—from behind the scenes like Katherine—provided the encouragement and inspiration to a brother, father, or husband in the aeronautics industry or personally contributed to the advance of aviation. Recent winners have included Fay Gillis Wells (2001), one of the first known female pilots; Evelyn Bryan Johnson (2002) for her work as a pilot, flight instructor, and aviation business leader; Eilene M. Galloway (2003) for her 45 years helping Congress on the legal issues of space law; and Gertrude Rogallo (2004) for helping her husband to create the "Rogallo wing," a cloth wing created in the late 1950s that gave birth to the sport of hang gliding.

As the popularity of bicycles grew, so did the Wright Cycle Company, located at 127 West Third Street in Dayton, Ohio.

The business expanded quickly and soon, the brothers had four bicycle shops in the area. Not content with just repairing them, Orville and Wilbur were soon designing their own models.

CHAPTER 3

To Reach the Sky

Although the bicycle business was booming, Orville and Wilbur were growing restless. In 1896, Orville contracted a potentially fatal disease called typhoid fever and for months, he was near death. The experience reminded both of the brothers how short and precious life was and only made their restlessness worse. "The boys of the Wright family are all lacking in determination and push," wrote Wilbur in a letter. "None of us has as yet made particular use of the talent in which he excels other men."[1] The newspaper headlines were full of stories about different men who were making gallant attempts to learn how to fly, and their bravery inspired Wilbur to find out more.

One day in June 1899, Wilbur sat down and wrote a letter to the Smithsonian Institution. He asked them to send him all the books and papers they had about the possibility of human flight. In his letter he wrote, "I have some pet theories as to the proper construction of a flying machine . . . I wish to avail myself of all that is already known and then if possible add my mite to help the future worker who will attain final success . . . I am an enthusiast, but not a crank."[2] The Smithsonian responded by sending a number of pamphlets and a list of recommended reading. The brothers read everything from cover to cover. They listened to the stories of the aviation experimenters around the world and soon, they caught the fever too.

As Orville and Wilbur learned more and more about the possibility of flight, they began to form their own ideas on how they

CHAPTER 3   To Reach The Sky

would approach creating their own flying machine. They quickly realized that the problem with many of the other machines was the lack of control. No flight could be safe if there was not a way to guide where the machine went while in the air. Soon they were discussing how to build one and as always, they threw ideas back and forth and plans began to form. Their years of working with bicycles had taught them different perspectives on balance. They knew that to keep balance, you had to move as one with the machine and perhaps that was a key that others had missed.

Asking their sister Katherine to take over the bicycle shops for a while, the brothers focused all of their attention on their new passion. Some of their inspiration for how the wings should be shaped and how to maintain balance in the air came from watching how birds flew. "My observations of . . . buzzards leads me to believe that they regain their lateral balance, when partly overturned by a gust of wind, by a torsion of the tips of their wings," wrote Wilbur.[3] Together, the brothers created a box kite with wings that were twisted in opposite directions. They called this process "wing-warping" and it was considered a truly revolutionary breakthrough in the development of controlled flight.

One of the books recommended by the Smithsonian was Octave Chanute's *Progress in Flying Machines*. The brothers began writing to Chanute and he replied immediately. He knew from that very first letter that these boys were something special. Over the course of the next ten years, Chanute and the brothers exchanged more than 400 letters. For Orville and Wilbur, Chanute was a role model, a mentor, and a sounding board for their new ideas and problems.

The first flying machine the brothers built in 1900 was made out of pinewood. The wings were covered in fabric and sealed with shellac. The wings spanned about five feet and were controlled by a set of cords just like a kite. Not satisfied with this model, they quickly built another

The Dawn of Aviation

one. This one was much bigger with a wingspan of almost seventeen feet. It too would be controlled from the ground. To test it properly, the brothers knew that they needed a very windy place. To find out the best spot, they contacted the U.S. Weather Bureau. They debated going to San Diego in California, as well as St. James in Florida but they finally decided to go to a beach on the outer banks of North Carolina. It was near a remote little fishing village called Kitty Hawk and it guaranteed steady winds and soft sand dunes for rough landings.

Wilbur explained to his father why they decided to go to Kitty Hawk over other locations. "I chose Kitty Hawk because it seemed the place which most closely met the required conditions. In order to obtain support from the air it is necessary . . . to move through it at the rate of 15 or 20 miles per hour . . . It is safer to practice in a wind, provided this is not too much broken up into eddies and sudden gusts by hills, trees and so forth," he continued. "At Kitty Hawk, which is on the narrow bar separating the Sound from the Ocean, there are neither hills nor trees, so that it offers a safe place for practice."[4]

While Kitty Hawk offered strong winds, it was not always the most pleasant place to be. The brothers were living right on the beach in tents. It was crawling with sand fleas and mosquitoes and the blowing sand sometimes buried the glider or sent it skittering across the beach. Sudden storms often blew across the ocean and hit the beach unexpectedly. In a letter home to Katherine, Orville wrote, "About two or three nights a week we have to crawl up at ten or eleven o'clock to hold the tent down. When one of these 45-mile nor'easters strikes us, you can depend on it, there is little sleep in our camp . . . We each had two blankets, but almost freeze every night," he continued. "The wind blows in on my head and I pull the blankets over my head, when my feet freeze, and I reverse the process. I keep this up all night and in the morning am hardly able to tell 'where I'm at' in the bedclothes."[5] The

CHAPTER 3   To Reach The Sky

bugs were often the worst of it and Orville wrote, "They chewed us clear through our underwear and socks! Lumps began swelling up all over my body like hen's eggs . . . Misery! Misery!"[6] Later, in his diary, he added, "The wind shaking the roof and sides of the tent sounds exactly like thunder. When we crawl out of the tent to fix things outside, the sand fairly blinds us."[7]

Despite some of the miseries of the place, the Wright Brothers enjoyed most of their time there immensely. They made quite a sight out on the beach. They always wore white shirts, suits, and ties and refused to fly on Sundays. The people of Kitty Hawk grew to respect them. John Daniels, one of regulars who helped the brothers, said, "They were two of the workingest boys I ever saw, and when they worked *they worked.* I never saw men so wrapped up in their work in my life. They

Reporters and other interested people often gathered around the brothers to watch them get the glider ready for flight.

These people could not believe what they were seeing. Would man actually fly? Could these quiet brothers have really achieved the impossible?

The Dawn of Aviation

had their whole heart and soul in what they were doing . . . ."[8] Both Wilbur and Orville experimented with the glider everyday possible, stopping only for winds to pick up or to fix something. They were helped by the Dan Tate family, the people who ran the Kitty Hawk post office. Mrs. Tate sewed the fabric for their glider's wings while Dan and his ten-year-old son Tom helped move the glider around and make repairs. Just before they left the beach in October 1900, Wilbur had his best rides of all. He covered more than 300 feet in less than 20 seconds. When the brothers packed up to return to Dayton, they left the glider on the beach. Mrs. Tate then took the material from the glider's wings and turned it into dresses for her daughters.

For three years in a row, the Wright Brothers returned to Kitty Hawk with gliders. They would fly, take notes, make changes and fly again. They took multiple photographs of the glider flights and developed them in their own darkroom. They would analyze each one for what could be done better the next time. They crashed a lot and got more than the average person's share of sand in their mouths, noses, eyes, and hair. They also learned some very valuable lessons about flight.

The brothers began to suspect that something was wrong with the air pressure tables they had been using. Although they were the official tables that everyone used, Orville and Wilbur believed they were not accurate. To find out, they decided to make a wind tunnel by placing a fan inside a washtub with the bottom cut out. The air rushed through a six foot long rectangular box and the brothers watched through a glass window on the top. They watched how the wind flowed around more than two hundred different shaped miniature wings and recorded their findings. From this, they not only created new air pressure tables but learned that rounded wings and curved propellers worked much better for pushing air.

CHAPTER 3   To Reach The Sky

Armed with this new information, Orville and Wilbur returned to Kitty Hawk once more in 1902 and this time, their glider worked even better. They also set up better shelters. Wilbur wrote, "We fitted up our living arrangements much more comfortably than last year. Our kitchen is immensely improved and then we have made beds on the second floor and now sleep aloft."[9] While they were there, their friend and mentor Chanute joined them with his own gliders. To his surprise, the Wright gliders flew much better than his! They made more than one thousand glides that year and two of them were over 600 feet.

The next step for the Wright Brothers was an obvious one: it was time to build a true flying machine. This time, it had a forty foot wingspan and was made primarily of spruce wood. For powered flight, they needed a light but powerful engine and for this, they turned to their bicycle mechanic, Charlie Taylor. He created a four-cylinder, twelve horsepower engine made out of cast aluminum. It was lightweight, weighing only 140 pounds. There was not another engine like it in the world. The flying machine, dubbed *The Flyer* by an optimistic Orville, had elevator wings in front, two rudders in back, and was steered through wires that twisted the main wings. The wings were covered in a fabric called muslin and the top and bottom wings were joined by nine pairs of struts and held by wires. A hip cradle was installed so that a pilot could lie flat and use the movement of his hips to control the rudder and wings. The front wings were managed with hand controls. The bottom of *The Flyer* did not have wheels like modern planes. Instead, it had skids like a sled. These would follow a sixty foot track put down on Big Kill Devil Hill, Kitty Hawk's largest dune.

Three years from the day they wrote to the Smithsonian Institution, the Wright Brothers were ready to attempt powered flight. Success was waiting just around the corner.

FYInfo
For Your Information

A LOOK AT THE COMPETITION

Leonardo da Vinci

Ever since Leonardo da Vinci came up with a drawing of a man with wings centuries ago, mankind has been fascinated by the ability to fly. As the end of the nineteenth century approached, more and more men were trying to find a way to take to the skies. The majority of them failed; while they might actually get off the ground, there was no way to control their flights. Crashes were commonplace. Otto Lilienthal from Germany was repeatedly in the news as he launched his glider off small hills more than 2000 times. He attempted to control it by shifting his body weight—not a safe or reliable method. Sadly, he died when a wind gust hit his glider and sent it out of control.

Hiram Maxim, the inventor of the portable machine gun, was busy building a giant steam-powered plane capable of flight. However, he was only able to get it a few inches off of the ground.

Perhaps the most famous of these brave men was Samuel P. Langley, secretary of the Smithsonian. He was fascinated by flight from an early age and could even be found sitting in the top of the tower at the National Zoological Park watching birds to see how they did it.

He attempted to fly in an aerodrome, a steam-driven fourteen-foot-long model plane. He was given $50,000 by the Smithsonian to fly and even received money from the United States Army. In 1903, he made two serious attempts in front of large crowds. Langley launched his machine off a houseboat on the Potomac River, near Washington D.C. Both times he plunged directly into the water and had to be rescued. Langley's aerodrome would one day turn into one of the Wright Brothers' biggest problems and eventually, they would all be involved in a legal fight.

Soaring over the ground at Kitty Hawk, *The Flyer* had a wingspan of just over 40 feet.

It featured many structural changes from the first gliders the brothers had built. Neither of them saw the whole thing put together until the parts were shipped from their bicycle shop to the Outer Banks and then assembled.

Success and Beyond

With *The Flyer* packed into multiple boxes and crates, the Wright Brothers headed back to Kitty Hawk in early autumn 1903. They were full of excitement and anxiety. Would their powered machine actually fly? Would they crash? Were they about to succeed or to fail? Would they live to tell about it?

Once they arrived, it took weeks to unpack and reassemble the parts into a working airplane again. Each day Orville and Wilbur would fiddle and tinker with the parts, while trying to tolerate the strong, cold winds. They wrote letters home almost every day, keeping their father and sister up to date on their progress.

The day of December 14, 1903 started out well. The brothers called for help from a group of people from Kitty Hawk to drag *The Flyer* up Big Kill Devil Hill. Orville and Wilbur flipped a coin to see who would be the one to take the first turn at making history and Wilbur won. He settled into the hip cradle, and he and *The Flyer* hurtled across the track. Unfortunately, the wind was coming from the side that day and the plane was crooked before it was airborne. There was too much lift and fifteen feet out, the plane stalled and crashed. Wilbur was uninjured but *The Flyer* needed repairs for broken parts. It took two long days to fix. Wilbur sent home a guardedly pleased message to Katherine and Milton which read, "We gave [the] machine [its] first test today . . . The machinery all worked in an entirely satisfactory manner and seems reliable . . . There is now no question of our final success."[1]

CHAPTER 4   Success and Beyond

December 17 was cold and the wind was blowing between 20 and 25 miles per hour. Nothing was going to stop the brothers now. This time only a handful of people showed up to help get *The Flyer* on its track. It was Orville's turn as pilot. At 10:35 a.m. the signal was given and he took off. Everyone held their breath as the plane came off the ground and for twelve monumental seconds flew through the air. John Daniels snapped a picture. It would one day be one of the most famous photographs in the world. Later in his life, he reflected on that moment. "I like to think about it now," he said. "I like to think about that first airplane the way it sailed off in the air at Kill Devil Hills . . . I don't think I ever saw a prettier sight in my life. Its wings and uprights were braced with new and shiny copper piano wires. The sun was shining bright that morning and the wires just blazed in the sunlight like gold. The machine looked like some big, graceful, gold bird sailing off into the wind . . . I think it made us all feel kind o' meek and prayerful like. It might have been a circus for some folks, but it wasn't any circus for us who had lived close by those Wright boys during all the months until we were as much wrapped up in the fate of the things as they were."[2]

After 120 feet, one of the skids caught in the sand and cracked. As *The Flyer* came to a halt all the men present knew one thing: man had just flown on a powered, controlled flight for the first time! It was a magical moment for the two brothers who had worked so hard for so long. At 11:20, Wilbur took a turn, this time flying 175 feet in fifteen seconds. Orville then flew 200 feet in the same amount of time. The last turn was the best; Wilbur soared 852 feet in 59 seconds. Triumphant, the brothers sent a telegram home to share the news with their family. It read:

> *Kitty Hawk, North Carolina   December 17*
> *Success four flights Thursday morning all against twent*
> *one mile wind started from level with engine power alone*

The Dawn of Aviation

average speed through air thirty one miles longest 57 seconds inform press home
Christmas   Orevelle Wright[3]

Even though there were errors in the telegram—the flight was 59 seconds, not 57 and Orville's name was spelled incorrectly—the important news was there. At long last, the Wright Brothers had accomplished what no one else had been able to do: sustained, powered, controlled flight.

It was time to go home. *The Flyer* was torn apart once again and put back into its crates and boxes for the trip back to Ohio. The brothers arrived home two days before Christmas. Although their family was delighted to see them and full of congratulations for what they had accomplished, the media was not as interested. All of the newspapers had been full of so many stories of people who almost flew for so many years that when they got another story about it, it was like the boy who cried wolf. They just didn't believe it and gave it little attention. Even though Katherine and Milton had sent news of the flight to the newspapers, their response was 59 seconds. Who cares? Most likely, it wasn't true anyway. It was probably another case of fliers that were liars.

The Wright Brothers were understandably disappointed, but that did not stop them from pursuing more knowledge about flight. They went to work building *The Flyer II*. Instead of returning to Kitty Hawk for further experiments, they found an open field eight miles from Dayton called Huffman Prairie. The field was actually a cow pasture and the farmer who owned it gave Wilbur and Orville permission to use it on one condition. They had to herd away the livestock before they began flying.

Once *The Flyer II* was ready in early 1904, the Wrights invited reporters out to Huffman Prairie to watch its trial runs. Although a

CHAPTER 4   Success and Beyond

number showed up, bad weather interfered and the longest flight was a mere thirty feet. Reporters went home unimpressed. In October, after the brothers made some modifications to *The Flyer II*, they invited reporters out to the cow pasture again. Few showed up but one that did was A. I. Root, a reporter for the journal *Gleanings in Bee Culture*. This flight went much better and Orville flew a total of twenty-four miles in thirty minutes. Root was astounded and one of the rare stories about the Wrights' first flights appeared in a bee magazine, next to articles such as "Judging Honey at Fairs" and "How I Manage Swarming." In January 1905, Root published, "Dear Friends, I have a wonderful story to tell you—a story that, in some respects, outrivals the *Arabian Nights* fables . . . it was one of the grandest sights, if not the grandest sight, of my life. Imagine a locomotive that has left its track, and is climbing up in the air right toward you—a locomotive without any wheels . . . but with white wings instead . . . a locomotive made out of aluminum. Well, now imagine this white locomotive, with wings that spread 20 feet each way, coming right toward you with a tremendous flap of its propellers, and you will have something like I saw."[4]

For three years, the Wright Brothers had been working on getting a patent on their flying machine and the special methods they had used to make it fly when others could not. While they waited, they refused to discuss or display its design with anyone and that frustrated the media. They had little interest in writing about this amazing machine that they knew almost nothing about.

Once the Wrights had their patent, they offered their plane and its technology to the U.S. Army. They were not interested. They felt the cost and danger of airplanes outweighed any benefits they might have. Unhappily, Orville and Wilbur then offered the information to the governments of France and England. They were definitely interested in what the Wrights had invented. For the rest of 1907 and into 1908,

The Dawn of Aviation

Wilbur flew their planes for a growing number of international crowds. Some numbered as large as 200,000 people and often included royalty. These flights were certainly not disappointing; Wilbur would swoop, turn, and do figure eights, showing a level of control no other flying machine ever had. They shattered all height, time, and distance records. At the same time, Orville was doing the same thing in Washington, D.C. As word spread, their fame grew. At long last, their story was put into print and the United States Army took notice.

Their success was marred in September 1908 when Orville lost control of one of his planes when the propeller broke. The plane crashed from a height of 150 feet. The accident killed his passenger, Lieutenant Thomas Selfridge, who had been a member of the Aerial Experiment Association and the official Army Aeronautics Board. Orville was also seriously hurt, with several broken ribs, a broken leg, and head and back injuries. Katherine quit teaching to take care of him as he recovered, but he would walk with a cane for the rest of his life and his family would say that he was never quite the same.

In May 1909, the brothers returned to the U.S., complete with trophies, rewards, and the love of Europe. To celebrate their return, the Wright Brothers were turned into celebrities with a hero's welcome. There were parades, concerts, and fireworks in their honor. Congress even awarded them a gold medal and they were guests at the White House. Not surprisingly, the U.S. Army decided to purchase a number of the Wrights' military flyers. Their requirements were that (1) the plane had to carry a pilot and a passenger; (2) fly at least 40 miles per hour; (3) stay aloft for at least one hour; (4) land without damage; (5) be portable and (6) be simple and quick to teach to new pilots. It was a deal!

As 1909 drew to a close, the Wright Brothers were doing well. They were being paid thousands of dollars to fly their planes in a variety

CHAPTER 4 Success and Beyond

of national events. They received $15,000 just for flying around the Statue of Liberty. In November, they opened the Wright Company where they planned to build their airplanes and teach others how to fly them. Quite unexpectedly, however, the nation's growing interest in flight turned in a new direction. As airplanes had the potential to fly higher and further, daring young men were finding ways to make money from them. For a price, men would do stunts in and on their planes, from daring dives to careful walks out on the wings while still in flight. The age of exhibition flying had been born. Even women were taking to the skies. Women wanted to fly too and some were not content being passengers. They wanted to pilot the planes themselves! It would be several years before a woman pilot would get a license but it would happen.

Not one to miss out on an opportunity, the Wright Brothers created the Wright Fliers Exhibition Team. A round trip flight from Philadelphia to New York was earning pilots a quick $10,000, equal to $195,000 today! Other fliers were paid $25,000 to fly round trip from New York to Chicago. Publisher and millionaire William Randolph Hearst even offered an amazing $50,000 to the pilot who could fly from coast to coast in under thirty days. Today that fee would be worth almost one million dollars!

The Wright brothers joined this get rich quick scheme for a while, and quickly earned more than a million dollars doing these tricks (worth $19.5 million today!) But, when five out of their nine pilots died in crashes, they changed their minds and shut down that part of their business.

FYInfo
For Your Information

WOMEN IN THE AIR

Imagine that you were one of the first women to ever actually fly up in the sky on an airplane! What would you worry about most? Motion sickness? Fear of heights? Whether the plane would fall apart way up in the air? For the ladies of the time period, their first concern was—their skirts.

Blanche Scott

The first woman to fly with the Wrights was the wife of one of their sponsors, Mrs. Hart O. Berg in France. She had seen Wilbur fly at Le Mans, France and had been completely captivated by it. She immediately asked him to take her for a ride. Afraid that the wind would blow her skirts so high that people would see her feet or legs, she tied a rope around them after taking a seat next to Wilbur. Her flight lasted two minutes and seven seconds and her skirt stayed in place. She was the first woman to fly. But Katherine's friend, Mrs. Ralph Van Doren, was the first woman to fly on American soil months later. Finally, in 1909, Orville and Wilbur thought it was time for Katherine to have her turn. All three women tied their skirts so there was no risk of anyone glimpsing an ankle.

A Parisian dressmaker saw photographs of these women walking away from the planes with their skirts still tied and was inspired. She designed a dress called a hobble skirt. It was long and narrow and went far below the knees. It was all the fashion between 1910 and 1914, even though women who wore them had to take very many short steps.

A mere two years later after the first woman went flying, the first female got in the pilot's seat. Her name was Blanche Scott and she had learned how to fly at Glen Curtiss's flying school. The following year, Harriet Quimby became the first American woman to get a pilot's license.

Glenn Curtiss was another man who wanted to conquer the skies.

He was a thorn in the side of the Wrights for years. Orville always believed that the stress from the relationship with Curtiss was a factor in his brother's death.

Protecting Patents and Winning Arguments

In many ways, the Wright Brothers by 1910 had everything they had ever wanted. The world had finally recognized their incredible contribution to aviation. In May, they took their elderly father up in the air and that same month, Orville and Wilbur shared the same plane for the very first time. The Wright Company, headquartered in New York was manufacturing two airplanes a month. Wilbur was president and Orville was the company's vice-president. It was his job to design and produce the world-famous flying machines. From 1910 to 1915, he created ten different types of planes. In the meantime, Wilbur was focusing on a much more complicated part of the business: protecting the Wrights' patents.

For years, aviation enthusiasts had contacted the Wright Brothers to ask questions and get some advice, just as they once did with their friend Chanute. It soon became obvious that some of these people were taking the information and using it to build their own planes. Using this information without permission was called copyright infringement. Wilbur filed a number of lawsuits against individuals and companies who he and Orville felt had illegally used some of their technology. One of these lawsuits was against the Aerial Experiment Association, a group formed by Alexander Graham Bell and included their long time rival, Glen Curtiss.

CHAPTER 5   Protecting Patents and Winning Arguments

Wilbur traveled a great deal during 1911 and 1912 in an attempt to keep up with the lawsuits. He found that the reputation of the Wright Brothers had changed in the world. Instead of being seen as brilliant, creative entrepreneurs, they were seen as greedy inventors who did not want to share their knowledge. This saddened both Orville and Wilbur and by the end of May 1912, Wilbur was slowing down. To the shock and dismay of everyone around him, he contracted typhoid fever and within a few days, he was dead at age 45. Milton wrote about his son in his diary. "A short life, full of consequences. An unfailing intellect, imperturbable temper, great self-reliance and as great modesty, seeing the right clearly, pursuing it steadfastly, he lived and died."[1]

Wilbur's death was very upsetting to Orville. They had been so close for so many years and he desperately missed his brother and partner. Cards and letters came in from all over the world expressing sadness for the loss of one of the world's most creative inventors.

Not long after Wilbur's death, the U.S. Circuit Court of Appeals agreed with the Wrights and declared that their patent was valid. This meant that anyone using their techniques of wind-warping and ailerons had to pay the Wrights a fee. The Wright Company stated they would deal with all companies kindly—except one. Glenn Curtiss, a long time rival, had caused Wilbur a great deal of stress and the Wrights felt he was a major contributor to Wilbur's death. To get back at the Wrights, Curtiss came up with a shocking plan. He contacted Charles Walcott, Langley's successor as secretary at the Smithsonian and asked permission to have the aerodrome that Langley had tried to fly a decade earlier taken out of storage. Curtiss wanted to restore it and then fly it, thus proving that the Wrights did not have the first machine capable of powered, controlled flight. He was given permission but while restoring it, Curtiss modified it, or made changes to the wings that reflected the Wrights' technology. When the aerodrome managed to make a few short

The Dawn of Aviation

5

It would be over 20 years before this famous glider plane would be given its place of honor in the museum.

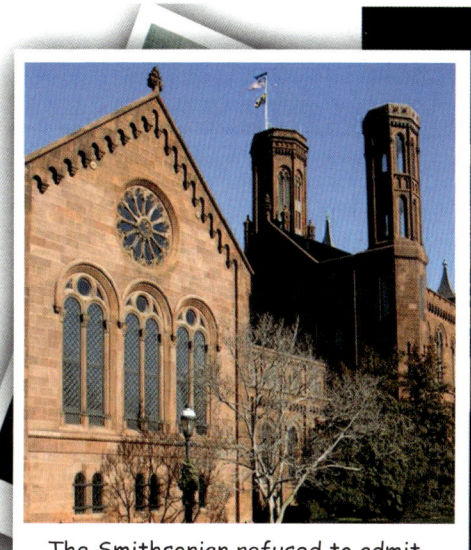

The Smithsonian refused to admit that *The Flyer* was the first design capable of a sustained flight.

flights, the Smithsonian announced that Langley had indeed built "the first man-carrying aeroplane in the history of the world capable of sustained free flight." Immediately, they displayed the aerodrome in their museum, instead of *The Flyer*.

Orville Wright was furious. He had to restore the honor and respect to their airplane but how would he convince the Smithsonian it was wrong? In September 1928, he wrote to Abbot. "If one wishes to continue to believe that the Langley machine was capable of flight in 1903 in spite of all evidence to the contrary he has the privilege of doing so," he wrote, "but no one has a right to lead others to this belief through false and misleading statements and through the suppression of the important evidence I have mentioned before."[2]

CHAPTER 5   Protecting Patents and Winning Arguments

Not knowing what else to do, Orville decided to take *The Flyer* and give it to the Science Museum in London instead. He felt bad that it would not be displayed in his own country, but felt he had little choice. "I believe that my course in sending our Kitty Hawk machine to a foreign museum is the only way of correcting the history of the flying machine, which by false and misleading statements has been perverted by the Smithsonian Institution," he wrote.[3]

As word got out about *The Flyer* going to England, Americans got angry. They wanted the plane to remain in the U.S. Soon Abbott was replaced by Charles Greeley and as the new secretary, he asked Charles Lindbergh, the pilot who flew his plane, *The Spirit of St. Louis*, solo from New York to Paris, to head a committee to work with Orville. He was unable to convince Orville to drop the issue. All Orville wanted was for the Smithsonian to admit that the aerodrome had been altered before it could fly and that their airplane was the first truly successful flying machine. The Smithsonian refused and so *The Flyer* went to London for four years. Throughout those years, Americans continued to write to the Smithsonian and ask them to change their minds.

In 1915, Orville sold his part of the Wright Company. He had been busy with the argument with the Smithsonian, and also working with the Dayton-Wright Airplane Company to produce British flight bomber planes. He stayed with them until 1923 when they went out of business. He was saddened to see that airplanes were being used as weapons in World War I. He once said, "I don't have any regrets about my part in the invention of the airplane, though no one could deplore more than I do the destruction it has caused."[4] By 1918, he was pleased to see that airplanes were being used for other purposes, such as locating forest fires, delivering mail, and dusting crops.

Orville was the guest of honor at many meetings and dinners and although he would show up, he refused to give a speech. The joker

The Dawn of Aviation

Lindergh was the first pilot to make a solo, non-stop flight from New York to Paris in 1927. He did it in thirty-three and a half hours.

Charles Lindbergh was one of the many well-known flyers to follow the Wright Brothers.

had become a quiet man in later years. In 1920, President Woodrow Wilson appointed Wilbur to the National Advisory Committee for Aeronautics. He received many awards, including eleven honorary degrees from several universities, the American Distinguished Flying Cross, and the French Legion of Honor. He continued to invent things including a clothes washer and a machine similar to a toaster.

As Orville got older, he spent much of his time in the home he had designed and built in Dayton. He called it Hawthorn Hill. His battle with the Smithsonian was still going on but finally, in 1942, the institution gave in and publicly published an article that stated *The Flyer* was, in fact, the first flying machine capable of sustained flight.

CHAPTER 5   Protecting Patents and Winning Arguments

Orville did not respond to the article and no one was sure what would happen next. It would be six years before the mystery was solved.

In October 1947, Orville had a heart attack. Months later, he had another and on January 30, 1948, the second of the Wright Brothers died. When his will was read, it stated that it accepted the Smithsonian's apology and gave *The Flyer* to the institution forever—unless it ever stated a different machine came before it.

On December 17, 1948, exactly 45 years after the Wright Brothers had their first successful flight, *The Flyer* was hung in the Smithsonian with great ceremony. On it was a plaque that read:

> *The original Wright Brothers' aeroplane*
> *The world's first power-driven*
> *Heavier-than-air machine in which man*
> *Made free, controlled and sustained flight*
> *Invented and built by Wilbur and Orville Wright*
> *Flown by them at Kitty Hawk, North Carolina*
> *December 17, 1903.*
> *By original scientific research the Wright Brothers*
> *Discovered the principles of human flight*
> *As inventors, builders and flyers they*
> *Further developed the aeroplane, taught man to fly, and opened*
> *The era of aviation.*[5]

Although multiple statues and plaques continued to be erected throughout the next several decades to honor the Wright Brothers, few were as massive and grand as the national monument built near Kitty Hawk. Standing sixty feet tall, it is made of granite with wings sculpted into the sides. Appropriately, it is mounted at the top of the 90-foot tall Kill Devil Hill dune. On the top sits a beacon that can be seen for miles—and naturally, by passing airplanes. It was dedicated on November 19, 1932 and the plaque on it reads:

5 The Dawn of Aviation

In commemoration of the conquest of the air by the brothers Wilbur and Orville Wright. Conceived by genius. Achieved by dauntless resolution and unconquerable faith.[6]

The age of aviation had truly begun with the Wright Brothers' invention. Two men, without advanced education, training, or even a high school diploma had accomplished what others could not. They dreamed of the skies, drew the designs, constructed the frames and finally, they touched the sky.

This was the site of many of the brothers' test flights with their gliders. It stands sixty feet tall and both brothers' names are carved into it.

The Wright Brothers National Monument is built on the top of a 90-foot dune named Big Kill Devil Hill.

FYInfo
For Your Information

THE AERIAL EXPERIMENT ASSOCIATION

Alexander Graham Bell

Another group fascinated by planes and how to build them formed in 1907. They were led by Alexander Graham Bell who, although best known for his invention of the telephone, was interested in many other things also, including flight. His wife Mabel was equally as fascinated by the possibilities and together, they contributed a great deal of money to the creation of an airplane. Bell, along with Glenn Hammond Curtiss, formed the new Aerial Experiment Association. Curtiss had already established quite a reputation for himself. He was known as "the fastest man in the world" because he had ridden a motorcycle at speeds of 136 miles per hour. Many experts believe he was the model for a series of children's books about a character called Tom Swift.

Together, Curtiss and Bell built three aircraft in three months: the *Red Wing*, the *White Wing*, and the *June Bug*. The third one was entered in a flying competition sponsored by Aero Club of America and *Scientific American* in 1908. Their plane set the official U.S. record for distance and won a huge trophy. The newspapers splashed it across front pages and when Wilbur found out about it, he was very angry. He stated that the Aerial Experiment Association's plane had used ailerons, small, triangular flaps on hinges attached to the top and the bottom of wings for additional control. This process, according to the Wright Brothers, was part of their patent only, and using them infringed on their rights. They had willingly shared information about their patented design with the group but under the agreement that it would not be used for flying in an exhibition or contest of any kind.

This was the first of many disagreements between the A.E.A. and the Wrights. Although the group dissolved in 1911, the ill feelings between the brothers and Curtiss would continue for years.

Chronology

1867	Wilbur Wright is born
1871	Orville Wright is born
1878	The Wright Brothers are given a toy helicopter
1889	The Wrights produce *West Side News* on their printing press
1892	The brothers open up a bicycle shop
1895	The Wright Cycle Company begins making bicycles
1899	Wilbur writes to the Smithsonian Institution for information on flight
1900	Orville and Wilbur begin testing gliders at Kitty Hawk
1901	The brothers continue testing gliders and create a wind tunnel
1903	*The Flyer* becomes the world's first flying machine capable of sustained flight
1904	*The Flyer II* is built and tested at Huffman Prairie, Ohio
1905	The brothers build *The Flyer III*
1907	Wilbur and Orville work to sell their airplanes to Europe
1908	Orville is injured and a passenger is killed in a flying accident
1909	The U.S. Army agrees to purchase *The Military Flyer*
1910	The Wright Brothers begin to do battle over patent infringements
1912	Wilbur dies
1915	Orville sells the Wright Company
1932	Wright Brothers National Memorial is dedicated at Kill Devil Hills
1942	The Smithsonian Institution issues an apology to Orville
1948	Orville dies; *The Flyer* is received into the Smithsonian Institution

Timeline in History

1854 George Cayley creates a glider that takes off successfully
1891 For five years, Otto Lilienthal is able to successfully guide gliders in flight
1903 The Wright Brothers make the first controlled, powered flight in *The Flyer* at Kitty Hawk
1915 The first fighter airplane is produced
1919 A successful transatlantic flight is done in 15 hours, 57 minutes
1927 Charles Lindbergh flies *The Spirit of St. Louis* from New York to Paris
1935 The first passenger airline is introduced in the United States
1939 In Germany the first flight of a jet-engine plane occurs
1947 A rocket-powered aircraft brakes the sound barrier
1957 *Sputnik 1*, a Soviet Union satellite, orbits the earth
1958 *Explorer 1*, an American satellite, is launched
1961 Yuri Gagarin and Alan Shepard fly into space
1969 Neil Armstrong and Buzz Aldrin walk on the moon
1971 Boeing 747 makes its first commercial flight from New York to London
1972 NASA announces the space shuttle program
1974 The SR-71 Blackbird sets the world speed record by flying across the Atlantic in 1 hour, 55 minutes, 42 seconds
1976 Concorde jets are introduced
1978 Americans Ben Abruzzo, Larry Newman, and Max Anderson make the first crossing of the Atlantic Ocean by hot air balloon
1981 The Space Shuttle Columbia begins it's first mission
1983 Sally Ride, an American female astronaut, becomes the first U.S. woman to go up into space
1987 The EH-101 helicopter is introduced
1999 Bertrand Piccard and Brian Jones become the first humans to circle the world in a hot air balloon
2003 Aviation celebrates its first century
2005 Steve Fosset accomplishes a solo nonstop flight around the world in just over 66 hours

Chapter Notes

Chapter One
A Simple Gift, A Grand Notion
1. The Franklin Institute, "Inventing the Future," http://www.fi.edu/flights/first/before.html
2. Russell Freedman, *The Wright Brothers: How They Invented the Airplane* (New York: Holiday House, 1991), p. 9.

Chapter Two
An Encouraging Environment
1. Wilbur Wright, April 2, 1912, in Marvin W. McFarland, ed. *The Papers of Wilbur and Orville Wright* (New York: McGraw-Hill, 1953), p. v.
2. Jane Yolen, *My Brothers' Flying Machine* (New York: Little, Brown, and Company, 2003), p. 1.
3. Fred C. Kelly's *The Wright Brothers: A Biography Authorized by Orville Wright* (New York: Harcourt-Brace, 1943), p.15.
4. Russell Freedman, *The Wright Brothers: How They Invented the Airplane* (New York: Holiday House, 1991), p. 10.
5. Ivonette Wright Miller, *Wright Reminiscences* (Ohio: The Air Force Museum Foundation, Inc., 1978), p. 61.

Chapter Three
To Reach The Sky
1. PBS, *The American Experience*, "The Wright Stuff," http://www.pbs.org/wgbh/amex/wright/transcript.html
2. *Century of Flight* (Virginia: Time Life Books, 1999), p. 31.
3. Judith E. Rinard, *Book of Flight* (New York: Firefly Books, 2001), p. 16.
4. Tom and Peter Jakab Crouch, *The Wright Brothers and the Invention of the Aerial Age* (Washington, D.C.: National Geographic, 2003), p. 70.
5. Judith E. Rinard, *Book of Flight* (New York: Firefly Books, 2001), p. 71.
6. Tom and Peter Jakab Crouch, *The Wright Brothers and the Invention of the Aerial Age* (Washington, D.C.: National Geographic, 2003), p. 70.
7. Elizabeth MacLeod, *The Wright Brothers: A Flying Start* (New York: Kids Can Press Ltd., 2002), p. 15.
8. James Tobin, *To Conquer the Air: The Wright Brothers and the Great Race for Flight* (New York: Free Press, 2003), p. 145.
9. PBS, *The American Experience*, "The Wright Stuff," http://www.pbs.org/wgbh/amex/wright/transcript.html

Chapter Four
Success and Beyond
1. George Sullivan, *The Wright Brothers* (New York: Scholastic, 2002), p. 5.
2. Noah Adams, *The Flyers: In Search of Wilbur and Orville Wright* (New York: Crown Publishers, 2003), p. 191.
3. Richard Maurer, *The Wright Sister: Katherine Wright and Her Famous Brothers* (Connecticut: Roaring Brook Press, 2003), p. 17.
4. NOVA, *Wright Brothers Flying Machine*, "The First Reporter," http://www.pbs.org/wgbh/nova/wright/reporter.html

Chapter Five
Protecting Patents and Winning Arguments
1. James Tobin, *To Conquer the Air: The Wright Brothers and the Great Race for Flight* (New York: Free Press, 2003), p. 362.
2. Tom and Peter Jakab Crouch, *The Wright Brothers and the Invention of the Aerial Age* (Washington, D.C.: National Geographic, 2003), p. 220-1.
3. Ibid, p. 224.
4. Elizabeth MacLeod, *The Wright Brothers: A Flying Start* (New York: Kids Can Press Ltd., 2002), p. 26.
5. Tom and Peter Jakab Crouch, *The Wright Brothers and the Invention of the Aerial Age* (Washington, D.C.: National Geographic, 2003), p. 232.
6. Ibid, p. 213.

For Further Reading

For Young Adults

MacLeod, Elizabeth. *The Wright Brothers: A Flying Start*. New York: Kids Can Press Ltd, 2002.

Old, Wendie. *To Fly: The Story of the Wright Brothers*. New York: Clarion Books, 2002.

Sullivan, George. The Wright Brothers. New York: Scholastic, 2002.

Yolen, Jane. *My Brothers' Flying Machine*. New York: Little, Brown and Company, 2003.

Works Consulted

Adams, Noah. *The Flyers: In Search of Wilbur and Orville Wright*. New York: Crown Publishers, 2003.

Century of Flight. Virginia: Time Life Books, 1999.

Crouch, Tom. *Wings: A History of Aviation from Kites to the Space Age*. New York: W. W. Norton, 2003.

Crouch, Tom and Peter Jakab. *The Wright Brothers and the Invention of the Aerial Age*. Washington, D.C.: National Geographic, 2003.

Freedman, Russell. *The Wright Brothers: How They Invented the Airplane*. New York: Holiday House, 1991.

MacLeod, Elizabeth. *The Wright Brothers: A Flying Start*. New York: Kids Can Press Ltd:, 2002.

Maurer, Richard. *The Wright Sister: Katherine Wright and her Famous Brothers*. Connecticut: Roaring Brook Press, 2003.

Rinard, Judith E., *Book of Flight*. New York: Firefly Books, 2001.

Sullivan, George. *The Wright Brothers*. New York: Scholastic, 2002.

Tobin, James. *To Conquer the Air: The Wright Brothers and the Great Race for Flight*. New York: Free Press, 2003.

Wright, Orville. Quoted in Fred C. Kelly's *The Wright Brothers: A Biography Authorized by Orville Wright*. New York: Harcourt-Brace, 1943.

Wright, Wilbur. April 2, 1912 in Marvin W. McFarland, ed. *The Papers of Wilbur and Orville Wright*. New York: McGraw-Hill, 1953.

Yolen, Jane. *My Brothers' Flying Machine*. New York: Little, Brown, and Company, 2003.

On the Internet

The Wright Brothers Aeroplane Company and Museum
http://www.wright-brothers.org/

Outer Banks of North Carolina, *Wright Brothers Memorial*
http://www.outerbanks.com/wrightbrothers/

PBS, *The Wright Brothers*
http://www.pbs.org/wgbh/nova/wright/

Glossary

Aeronautics (AIR-oh-NAW-tiks)
the design and construction of aircraft

Ailerons (AY-la-RONS)
either of two movable flaps on the wings of an airplane that can be used to control the plane's rolling and banking movements

Congregations (CON-gra-GAY-shuns)
group of people gathered for religious worship

Copyright infringement (COPY-rite en-fringe-ment)
violation of the rights secured by a copyright

Granite (GRAH-nit)
common, coarse-grained, light-colored, hard igneous rock

Imperturbable (EM-pur-tur-ba-BULL)
extremely calm and collected

Muslin (MUZ-len)
any of various sturdy cotton fabrics of plain weave, used especially for sheets

Patent (pa-TENT)
a grant made by a government that confers upon the creator of an invention the sole right to make, use, and sell that invention for a set period of time

Optimistic (OPT-o-MISS-tik)
one who usually expects a favorable outcome

Shellac (sha-LACK)
a thin varnish used to seal seams or finish wood

Skitter (SKIT-TER)
to scamper, or move quickly across the ground

Tuberculosis (Too-berk-you-LOH-sis)
an infectious disease of the lungs of humans and animals

Typhoid fever (TIE-foyd FEE-ver)
an acute, highly infectious disease transmitted chiefly by contaminated food or water

Index

Aerial Experiment Association 31, 35, 42
American Distinguished Flying Cross 39
Bell, Alexander Graham 42
Berg, Mrs. Hart O. 33
Big Kill Devil Hill 24, 27-28, 40
Chanute, Octave 20, 23, 35
Curtiss, Glen 33, 34, 36, 42
Da Vinci, Leonardo 25
Daniels, John 22, 28
Dayton-Wright Airplane Company 38
Flyer, The 23-24, 26, 27, 28-29, 37
Flyer II, The 29-30
French Legion of Honor 39
Gates Learjet Corporation 17
Gauchot, Paul 9
Gleanings in Bee Culture 30
Greeley, Charles 38
Hawthorn Hill 39
Hearst, William Randolph 32
Hobble skirt 33
Huffman Prairie 30
Kitty Hawk 21-22, 23, 26, 27, 40
Langley, Samuel P. 25, 36
Lindbergh, Charles 38, 39
Lilienthal, Otto 25
Maxim, Hiram 25
National Advisory Committee For Aeronautics 38-39
Penaud, Alphonse 8, 9
Planophore 9
Progress in Flying Machines 20
Quimby, Harriet 33
Root, A. I. 30
Science Museum in London 37
Scott, Blanche 33
Selfridge, Lt. Thomas 31
Sines, Ed 13
Smithsonian Institution 19-20, 24, 25, 36, 37, 38, 39, 40
Spirit of St. Louis, the 38
Tate, Dan 22
Tate, Mrs. 22
Tate, Tom 22
Taylor, Charlie 23
Typhoid fever 19, 36
U.S. Army 31
Van Doren, Mrs. Ralph 33
Walcott, Charles 36
West Side News, The 14
Wilson, President Woodrow 38
Wind tunnel 23
Wright Brothers National Monument 40-41
Wright Company 32
Wright Cycle Company 15, 18
Wright Fliers Exhibition Team 32
Wright, Ida 12
Wright, Katherine 7, 14, 17, 20, 21, 27, 29, 33
   Memorial Award 17
Wright, Lorin 7, 12
Wright, Milton 7, 11, 27
Wright, Orville
   birth of 12
   crash 31
   death of 40
   first flight 28
   letters 21-22
   sold Wright Company 38
   telegram 29
   typhoid fever 19
Wright, Otis 12
Wright, Reuchlin 7, 12
Wright, (Koerner) Susan 11, 14
Wright, Wilbur
   birth of 12
   building kites 13
   contacts Smithsonian 19
   death of 36
   flying for international crowds 31
   traveling for lawsuits 35
   Yale University 14